CON

PARIS TOUJOURS PARIS

THE NINE LIVES OF GABRIELLE: FOR THREE SHE STRAYS - BOOK 1

LAURA MARIANI

THE PEOPLE ALCHEMIST

ABOUT THE AUTHOR

Laura Mariani is an Author, Speaker and Entrepreneur.

She started her consulting business after a successful career as Senior HR Director within global brands in FMCG, Retail, Media and Pharma.

Laura is incredibly passionate about helping other women to break through barriers limiting their personal and/or professional fulfilment.

Her best selling nonfiction *STOP IT! It is all in your head* and the *THINK, LOOK & ACT THE PART* series have been described as success and transformation 101.

She is a Fellow of the Chartered Institute of Personnel & Development (FCIPD), Fellow of the Australian Human Resources Institute (FAHRI), Fellow of the Institute of Leadership & Management (FInstLM), Member of the Society of Human Resources Management (SHRM) and Member of the Change Institute.

She is based in London, England with a strong penchant for travel and visiting new places.

She is a food lover, ballet fanatic, passionate about music, art, theatre. She likes painting and drawing (for self-expression not selling but hey, you never know...), tennis, rugby, and of course fashion (the Pope is Catholic after all).

www.thepeoplealchemist.com
@PeopleAlchemist
instagram.com/lauramariani_author

NEW FICTION OUT ON 12 JULY

THE NINE LIVES OF GABRIELLE: FOR
THREE SHE STRAYS - BOOK 2

ME MYSELF *and* Us

LAURA MARIANI

ALSO OUT 12 JULY

THE NINE LIVES OF GABRIELLE:
FOR THREE SHE STRAYS - BOOK 3

Freedom over Me

LAURA MARIANI

NEW NON-FICTION BY LAURA MARIANI

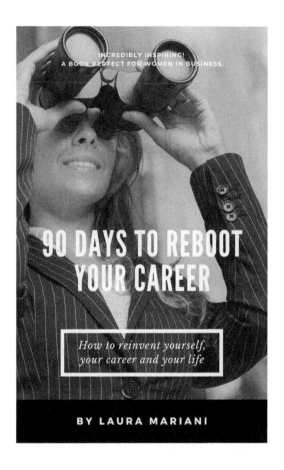

INCREDIBLY INSPIRING!
A BOOK PERFECT FOR WOMEN IN BUSINESS.

90 DAYS TO REBOOT YOUR CAREER

*How to reinvent yourself,
your career and your life*

BY LAURA MARIANI

ALSO BY LAURA MARIANI

Fiction

For Three She Plays - Book 1 - 3

A New York Adventure

Troubled after the break-up of a long term relationship, Gabrielle sets out for a sabbatical in New York.

A travelogue searching for self, pleasure and fun. And the Big Apple doesn't disappoint.

Searching for Goren

Why are we always choosing people who don't allow intimacy? Is it because deep down we don't want it?

Tasting Freedom

As her trip to New York comes to an end, her shackles bare falling and Gabrielle begins to taste, finally, freedom.

Non-Fiction

STOP IT! It is all in your head

The RULE BOOK to Smash The infamous glass ceiling -

For women & young women everywhere —

personal transformation & success 101.

The Think, Look & Act The Part Series.
Think The Part

Upgrade your consciousness and mind-set.

Make winning a key part of your life and business.

Look The Part

Upgrade your personal brand.

Make presenting your unique Best Self a key part of your life and business.

Act The Part

A personal coach to act in spite of fear, right here, right now.

More non-fiction books and courses are coming soon. For new releases, giveaways and pre-release specials check www.thepeoplealchemist.com

You can also buy my books and courses directly from me at www.payhip.com/LauraMariani

ThePeopleAlchemist Press publishes self help, inspirational and transformational books, resources and products to help #TheWomanAlchemist in every woman to change her life/career and transmute any circumstance into gold, a bit like magic to **Unlock Ignite Transform.**

ISBN: 978-1-915501-10-3

To Paris, one of my three loves

"PARIS IS ALWAYS A GOOD IDEA"
- **AUDREY HEPBURN**

PARIS TOUJOURS PARIS

PROLOGUE

S elf-Image is our self-limiting portable box.
 Our world and everything in it reflects our mental attitude toward ourselves.

It's the ultimate internal regulator: whenever the temperature rises above comfort level, it will take us back to base like a thermostat. Self-image is determined by the paradigms that run our life and mind unconsciously.

Unless we resolve our deep-rooted issues, address our core needs and then up-level our self-image, we will reach the "temperature" we are comfortable in sooner or later.
 Then Self-sabotage comes in.

And there we start again.

. . .

And sometimes, we cross the line and our moral compass to meet our needs.

Laura xxx

G abrielle woke up, the sun filtering through the gap in the heavy curtains.

They were back home after a long weekend celebrating. Celebrating in more ways than one.

The day before, after dinner and the night at the Opera, Gabrielle had finally started to open up to Mr Wonderful. They were out to celebrate the day they met—another of the many surprises from Mr Wonderful.

He was still asleep, and she couldn't stop looking at him, fearing he would disappear like a *mirage.* How lucky she was.

And how afraid she was going to screw this up too.

Mr Wonderful lips were slightly arched as if whatever he was dreaming of made him smile. His thick dark eyebrows were framing his masculine face perfectly. A strand of hair covering his forehead and just a little stubble from a few days without shaving covering his face. He smelled soo good: a mixture of his cologne and after-sex pheromones. His arms were still around her, as he couldn't quite sleep without being close to her, skin to skin.

He was very handsome and, from his facial expressions, looked like he was having a perfect dream.

Gabrielle was lying there, motionless, trying not to breathe, not to wake him up. Precious moments. She loved them and savoured them. No questions asked. Just contemplating how lucky she was. Especially after talking, aka talking about herself. They spent the previous day talking, or at least it had felt like a day to Gabrielle.

She had to.

She had spent the whole time whilst they were at dinner and the Opera wondering in and out of her consciousness, back and forward from her past. And he had noticed. Of course.

He was always so attentive. "Too much sometimes", thought Gabrielle. She'd prefer if he couldn't read her so well. What she had always craved was here, and it was not as easy as she had hoped. Intimacy is a bummer.

She always liked to present the best of herself. The best of herself she wanted the world to see. Being laid bare was excruciating.

"Good morning, gorgeous",

Mr Wonderful said, flashing one of his dazzling smiles. Perfect pearly whites. His blue eyes pierced through her soul.

"Good morning",

She purred and sunk her face into his chest, trying not to look into his eyes.

He knew she had done enough talking, at least for now, far more than she was used to, so he held her firmly, stroking her back whilst kissing her forehead.

"I love you",

Mr Wonderful whispered, "Always".

Gabrielle looked up for a minute and replied,

" I love you too, more than I can say".
"I know".

They stayed in bed some more, lingering.
The crumpled bed sheets around them.

After some time had passed, she got up and started getting ready for her morning walk. One of the few habits she developed during lockdown that she kept after starting her relationship with Mr Wonderful. You can't exactly run an overnight tape with 'I am a Goddess' affirmations when you are sleeping next to someone you are remotely interested in— or can't sleep either with one of those gizmos with Bluetooth, still not very sexy.

But she kept the morning walks and writing her morning pages. She started carrying a notebook with her on her walks and stopped from time to time to write her thoughts. Whatever came to mind: anything and everything.

Mr Wonderful was a gym type of person, so she used that time to do her own thing.

"Darling, I need to write some papers for work. Do you mind if I use your office?" he asked.

Ever so polite, he understood how precious Gabrielle was with her space, house, and things. Between falling deeply in love and lockdown, they practically moved in together almost immediately, and he was wary of not "overstepping" and being overfamiliar. He was determined not to take anything for granted.

"Not going to the gym?" Gabrielle asked.

"Maybe after I finish work, I have a deadline".

"Sure, I am going for a walk".

"I'll be here", Mr Wonderful replied.

Gabrielle always enjoyed walking, especially down the canal. Being near the water, the sounds and the smell made her feel at peace and relaxed. She often stopped and sat to write her morning pages whilst watching the canal and the locals going on with their daily life.

The water was standing still...

"Be still and know that I...," peacefully meditating in the moment.

The door closed behind Gabrielle, and Mr Wonderful jumped out of bed and into a quick shower before getting ready to do some work.

With a fresh cup of coffee in his hand, he then proceeded towards the small crook in the corner of the house that Gabrielle had designated as an office. There it was where Gabrielle did all her work, painting, writing and filming for her YouTube channel. A foldable antique lacquered screen was concealing the area.

. . .

Clear boundaries,

"So Gabrielle," he thought as he folded the screen away and sat at the desk.

He powered up his laptop, checked his emails and then the stock exchange, followed by a quick call to his broker to sell and buy some stock and shares. The desk was just by the window, looking over Canonbury Square and Canonbury Gardens.

He found himself wondering.

Wondering how hard he had fallen for her and how fast.

How she walked into his life out of the blue. He had never met anybody before this enchanting, enthralling, and so elusive.

His previous long-term relationships had always played the second field to his business and personal interests: cars, racing, and flying. And now, all he wanted was Gabrielle.

Her big brown eyes had captivated him from the first moment; her perfume seduced him, and her voice sealed the deal.

But, most of all, it was her sweetness and vulnerability hiding behind the strong, badass facade.

. . .

Yes, she was beautiful, almost hypnotising, even more, because she was playing it down and self-deprecating. She didn't fully realise the effect she had on men, or on him. When she walked into a room …

"Boy, I have fallen hard," he thought.

"I need paper. Where does she keep printing paper?" he asked himself.

He looked into a few drawers of Gabrielle's exquisite French cabinet which she used as a desk.

"Nope", pens, highlighters, pencils, brushes but no paper. "Ah, here it is," he said as he opened the last drawer.

As he took the A4 paper out of the drawer, he noticed something that looked like a folded note. Maybe something Gabrielle had written recently ...

"I shouldn't look", he thought, reminding himself how private she was.

But the letter bated, called him and tempted him to read it. For hours he resisted and kept on working. But he couldn't concentrate, he was distracted. The letter kept popping into his mind.

. . .

Then, finally, he gave in; he made another cup of coffee, sat down and unfolded the inviting note.

"*Ma chérie Gabrielle, n'aie pas peur de combien je te désire*".

Mr Wonderful French was rusty, but he understood a few core words like "*désire*". He searched for Google Translate on his laptop and typed the words with apprehension.

"Dear Gabrielle, don't be afraid of how much I desire you", read the first line.

His heart was sinking, and his mind was going awry.

"When was it written? Where is the date? There is no date in this letter," he thought.

He cursed himself for not paying more attention to the French classes in school and not practising more French with Gabrielle. The process of translating phrase by phrase was excruciatingly painful.

So slow. Mr Wonderful's mind was playing with his heart when he noticed that Gabrielle was standing right there, looking at him looking at her, the letter unfolded in his hands.

Gabrielle couldn't help but notice his expression, the colour had drained from his face.

Gone was the loving look he had earlier on.

Instead, Mr Wonderful looked stone-faced, almost grey; his eyes were red and swollen.

. . .

"Has he been crying?" she thought. "What is he reading?".

It was then she noticed the open drawer where she kept THE letter. *Le PDG* wrote it to her when he feared that their love affair was doomed to end, and soon.

Paris, Toujours, Paris taunting her.

After the New York sabbatical, Gabrielle felt reinvigorated with a new perspective on life. In the last month in the Big Apple, she had thoroughly worked on herself and done some introspection.

Gabrielle had always shied away from getting too deep into anything: relationships, herself, life. She never understood how she always stopped on the verge of greatness, on the brink of enormous success.

Something always happened, somehow, and she couldn't see the pattern. But now, everything looked so painfully clear. Too painful. Gabrielle had so many shields and layers that she wasn't just protecting herself from the world. She was keeping herself from the world.

Back in London, in familiar places, everything however looked so different. She remembered escaping from her "village" and arriving in London only to confine herself to another "village", barely getting out of it. A self-imposed upgraded cage, which now was feeling claustrophobic.

Gabrielle was back at work and ready for new challenges. Work had always been her safe place, where her achievements spoke for themselves with her identity firmly rooted in them. Work had been her life.

Her phone rang.

"Did you have a good time?"

Her MD asked.

"Yes, thanks, fabulous!"

She replied.

"Are you going all American on me now?"

He smirked. "Can I see when you have a minute?".

"Sure, I have a gap in my schedule after lunch. Sheryl has already planned my life for the next decade",

Gabrielle said.

"Yes, your P.A. is very efficient. After lunch, it is fine".

Gabrielle caught up with emails and read the summary prepared for her. Sheryl had been sifting through her emails while Gabrielle was away and diverting them to the appropriate member of her team.

"What would I do without my Sheryl?" she said.

After looking at the latest report on market share and preparing for the meetings in the afternoon, Gabrielle took some time for lunch.

She could have easily met the MD over that hour, but her P.A. had made a point of blocking time so she could take care of herself, eat properly and not just gulp something down whilst talking about work. She was behaving more like her mother every day.

Knock, knock...

"Come in", the MD said. "Coffee?".
    "Yes, please," said Gabrielle.

"When you were in New York, lots of changes happened, some moves, some people left", he started, clearing his throat.

"Yes, I know; Sheryl has filled me in. I have seen the announcement for the departure. Interesting", she replied.

"Usual announcement in this type of case", implying this particular one hadn't been a 'voluntary' leaver.

"Well, with all these changes", he proceeded, "there are now empty positions, you know ... opportunities", looking at Gabrielle intensely.

"I imagine so", she said. The penny hadn't dropped yet.
    "What's going on with you?" he asked. "What happened in New York? You would have knocked at my door. Hell, putting it down to talk to me about opportunities before".

She squinted her eyes.

"Well, never mind. There is a permanent position opening in Paris, working with the main Board of Directors for the Group and *Le PDG* But the role is based in France. What do you think?"

Gabrielle was happy to be back at work and in her element but, for once in her life, she hadn't quite thought or planned her next move.

At least not yet.

"I love Paris. It sounds interesting. I just bought my house in London",

She said tentatively, thinking a permanent move to France was not exactly what she had anticipated.

"You know the company helps with relocation, finding a place and so on..."

"Yes, I know".

"So, what do you think?" he repeated.

Gabrielle knew that if you truly wanted to advance your career in the company, you had to both go and handle the acquisition and integration of a new company into the Group, the French way, and have worked in France. At least for a bit.

. . .

They were the unspoken rules. Paired with the other unspoken rule that all company directors throughout the Group have to speak French.

Although English was the commercial language of the Group, if you met *Le PDG* or present to him and the Board, you did so in French.

"If you are interested, they are interviewing next week in Paris. First, second and third interview on the same day".

"Validating?" she kind of asked, but not really.

"Yes, that's right. Validating".

Gabrielle knew French working culture well and the politics that come with that. It was the differentiating factor that got her job role: that and the fact she was bilingual. Gabrielle was working as Marketing and PR Director for the Group branch in the UK, the not-so-unspoken rebel.

France wanted the UK branch to be managed the French way, but the UK was having none of it. They needed an in-betweener to bridge the cultural gap.

"Why don't you leave then? "
    Gabrielle said during a UK board meeting to one of her colleagues, the Sales Director.

Everybody turned to look at her, astonished that she had said that aloud.

The Sales Director was a middle-aged Scottish man who had worked for the company for twenty years; ten before the company was acquired by the French Group.

In ten years, despite lessons, he still couldn't string two French sentences together. Gabrielle had lost her (French) patience with him.

He was not feeling appreciated, blah blah blah ... the French this, blah blah... the French that, blah blah blah...

"If you don't like it, why don't you leave?"
    She repeated.

"In this day and age, companies should recognise their employees", he kept on moaning.

"You are not an employee. You are a Board Director. And that's not the culture! This is a French company. More direct, *combative* and with far less sugar coating. You are expected to do well. It is a bit like school and parents going to meet their children's teacher to find out how they are doing. The teacher will not sing the child's praises and tell the gushing mother how wonderful the child is.

. . .

Non, the teacher will point out what the child is not doing well. Because they are expected to do well within the confinements of their age group. Same as you are expected to do well in a job you get paid handsomely to do.

You are not going to get praised for it too.

Get over it".

They all looked at her like she had just made a significant revelation.

"Sorry all, but that's the way it is."

Gabrielle was so French when in London and so British when in France.

Politics and all the sycophants that worked with *Le PDG* was something she would need to get used to pretty fast.

The Group Board of Directors was a mix of old schoolmates of *Le PDG* or people who had risen through the ranks from when his father was at the company's reign.

He had grown the company from a small artisan one in the north of France to one of the most prominent in the country, and now, *Le PDG* had expanded it globally, acquiring an average of one or two companies per year, every year.

Gabrielle was presenting for the first time to *Le PDG* in her new capacity and wanted to make an impression.

· · ·

She had researched the subject thoroughly and prepared stats and figures to back up her proposed strategy. Her presentation was in English, but all the handouts were in French, and she presented in French. She dressed up for the occasion, too: more feminine than she would have in London but pared down, letting her mind do the talking.

The office was in *Tour Montparnasse* with a spectacular view of the *Tour Eiffel*.

The room was set up in a traditional presentation style with *Le PDG* placed right in the middle of the table, his right-hand and left-hand men on each side, and then in order of importance and inner circle closeness.

He was known in the company for asking many questions; the unspoken rule to anyone presenting to him was 'know your figures or suffer the consequences'.

"A bit dramatic", she thought, but she memorised all the figures and handouts nevertheless. Just in case.

Le PDG was in his early forties and had been leading the company for at least ten years, the sole shareholder of a private now multi-billion euros company.

He was tall and slender, wearing tortoise glasses resting on his long aquiline nose. His hair was mousy, with a hint of grey running through his temples.

He was notoriously private, so much so that there weren't any pictures of him in circulation, much to the dismay of the French press.

· · ·

His anonymity allowed him to travel between *Londrienne* and Paris on the TGV on his own, unnoticed.

Le PDG looked at Gabrielle intensely as she entered the room. Gabrielle had sent copies of her presentation and collateral in advance and expected a grilling.

And she got one.

He interrogated her for hours, the only one asking the questions. All the others nodded, making the obligatory "*Oui, oui*" noises from time to time.

Gabrielle stood there, defiant, answering every question without hesitating. She had memorised every page and every figure and tried to pre-empty every question he might have.
It was a duel — a hypnotic duet they were playing.

His eyes never once left hers.
Penetrating hers.

And at the end "*Bon*". And the meeting was over.

As everyone started to get up and leave the room, he said:
"We are going for lunch now. Would you like to join us?".
Gabrielle wondered if this happened all the time, but this wasn't the time for questioning. "*Oui, merci*," she said.

. . .

They all left and went down the elevator for what seemed like an eternity.

The company office was based on the 55th floor, just below the observation deck on the 56th and the rooftop garden on the 59th.

Le PDG was standing right next to her, towering over her. He was intent on conversing with one of the others, but she could feel the warmth of his body.

The descent went slowly, with a stop on almost every floor. And with more people coming in, the lift was feeling more and more snuggling. *Le PDG* closer and closer.

As they walked out of the building, he started walking beside her and making small talk nonchalantly. Next, they went to one of the restaurants in the area for lunch.

He sat next to her and then talked with everyone around the table but Gabrielle.

She did the same.

As they were all chatting, their arms touched, at first, occasionally and unintentionally.

Then, as the lunch went on, more and more. Gabrielle looked around to see if anyone at the table was paying attention, but they all seemed oblivious and immersed in the food experience.

· · ·

When back in the office, Gabrielle composed herself in the ladies' room.

"What are you doing? He is THE boss, and he is married",
    She said, looking into the mirror.
    "Nothing, I'm doing nothing. It was only lunch. It meant nothing".

But it did. It meant something indeed.
    Things capitulated from there.

The next time they met was at a tasting for a new product line. A room full of people, but they could only see each other. They were inevitably drawn to one another, each trying to overcome their fallacies and the incongruences the situation posed to both.

Gabrielle still remembered what it felt like finding out she was the other woman with the Stud. She felt physically sick.

And *Le PDG* was a good catholic boy who had been married to his childhood sweetheart for the last twenty years. He was living in Paris, Mondays to Fridays, and travelling back to *Londrienne* to spend the weekend with his wife and their three children.

Paris was not for her, the wife; she had lived in her small town all her life and had never wanted to leave. Paris was too much for her.

She enjoyed the quiet life, meeting with her friends for lunch whilst the children were at school. He was her security and validation.

Everyone in town, in one way or another, was connected to her husband's company, and she revelled in that.

He always wanted to travel and conquer the world, and his work allowed him just that.

And he did take the world by storm; nobody believed he could carry the company when his father died, let alone make it a global multi-billion euros one.

So he married young because it was expected to do; their families intertwined. And she was a good wife. Better still, she was loyal and invisible.

Gabrielle, on the other hand, was everything he wanted. She was equally driven, pushing herself all the time.

He wanted her but wasn't one hundred per cent sure she would reciprocate. He thought all the signs were there, but she was a puzzle.

Gabrielle was equally attracted, like the moth to the fire but wasn't quite sure he wanted her enough to do anything about it. And he was married.

So they played their dance, sussing each other out, a life argentine tango.

And then one day, everything changed.

· · ·

"Hello Madame, *Le PDG* wants to go through the new strategy and the budget; he has an opening tomorrow at 4.00 pm",

his Executive Assistant said over the phone.

"I'll have to move a meeting", Gabrielle said.

"Please do", she replied.

Gabrielle was nervous and re-looked at the presentation and her figures over, wondering what was wrong.

But, everybody seemed to have liked it and the decision to progress it had been made. She went over the information over and over for the rest of the day and evening and then the next day too.

She had just moved to Paris and was still finding her feet in her new role.

The meeting time came when the EA called to say he was going to be late; his previous meeting had overrun. Gabrielle took her time to compose herself and do a quick touch-up with some blush and a veil of lipstick, just as if she had just bitten her lips.

4.30 went by.

It was 4.45 when the EA called her in.

• • •

"Please sit down", as he showed her the chair on the other side of his desk.

"Sorry I am late".

"It's ok," she said and couldn't think of anything else. She certainly couldn't say she was pissed off for having waited almost an hour.

They started going over the figures for the budget, and the phasing of those figures and time seemed to get by quickly when there was a knock at the door.

"Monsieur, I'm going home. Do you need anything?" his EA said.

"No, it's all right, thank you. Have a nice evening".

Gabrielle hadn't realised they had been talking for over two hours, and it was now almost seven p.m., and they were the only ones left in the office.

He stood up by the window, looking at the lit Tour Eiffel.
    Gabrielle stood silently, not quite knowing what to do or say.

"You can see most of Paris from here. Beautiful, isn't it?"

He said, turning to look at her.

"Yes, it is",
She replied, thinking how banal her response was, 'Yes, it is. Couldn't I have said something more interesting?'

He turned his back again and continued to look outside. She wasn't sure if that was an invitation to join him. She decided it was. He wasn't looking like he wanted to return and continue talking business.

She started walking towards him slowly, unsure if it was the right thing on many levels. As she was moving forward, he turned and looked at her intensely, savouring her every move.

Today was the day; he couldn't hold his feelings any longer. He had to know if she felt the same.

Now.

"You are beautiful",
He said, thinking how stupid and how vulnerable he was making himself right now. She could complain.

Worse, she could reject him. But he couldn't wait another minute.
He had to know.

. . .

"I have been unable to stop thinking about you; I just wanted to see you alone. Sorry for keeping you at work late",
He whispered.

Gabrielle didn't know how to react. The feminist in her should have felt at least some indignation, but she didn't. The moralist in her should have been repelled, but she wasn't. Instead, she just wanted to...

And then he kissed her. Slowly and gently at first.

Her forehead, her cheeks and then her mouth. A moment suspended in time. Or so it seemed.

Hours spent kissing. They finally walked out of the office around nine o'clock. He walked her home, up to her door, and kissed her goodnight.

Gabrielle couldn't sleep that night. He had bypassed her barriers and gone straight to her core.

She tossed and turned and then watched the sun rise.

She was excited to go to work and took particular care in getting ready and found herself skipping down the pavement.

. . .

Gabrielle couldn't wait to see *Le PDG* again. When she arrived at the office, the door was shut, and the light was off.

"Strange", she thought.
  Hours went by, and nothing.

No sign of *Le PDG.*

She heard in passing that he was travelling out of the country for an acquisition, and he won't be back until the following week. Gabrielle felt her face becoming red and had to go and collect herself.

"Stupid, stupid, did you think that he was going to tell you?"
  She said, looking in the mirror.

Nevertheless, tears started to fill up her eyes. She took some time before returning to her desk and then shut the door for the rest of the day.

The week passed by slowly and uneventfully. Gabrielle was still decorating her new Paris apartment. She had decided not to sell her London home and was commuting each weekend.
  Going back to London was just what she needed right now; she couldn't face her empty Paris apartment, alone.

. . .

The following week came by, and her diary was filled with meetings with various board members, other directors and *Le PDG*.

She couldn't help but feel anger and resentment rising, the genie was out of the bottle now, and she was struggling to put her back.

They saw each other several times with other people, and she caught him staring at her when the others weren't looking.

However, he had made no effort to contact her outside work or see her alone. Gabrielle was thinking she was delusional, that she had imagined the whole thing, until …

Until they met again. This time alone.

"How are you?" he asked.

"Fine",

She said sternly, "How can I help?"

As if nothing had happened. But it had. He drew closer and closer until their bodies touched.

"I missed you", he said

"I didn't want to miss you. I was trying not to. But I did", he whispered in her ear.

"Did you miss me?"

"Nope"

"Not even a little bit?"

He started kissing her. "Gabrielle, baby, say something".

She wanted to push him away but couldn't resist him. She kissed him back. They soon were all over each other, on his desk, by the window. He had locked the door, but people knew better than disturbing when he was in meetings.

From then on, they grabbed every moment they could.

Anywhere and everywhere during the day. And in the evenings, cooking and making love in her apartment.

They ached for each other.

Their passion was a spectacular affirmation of two minds struggling past their incongruences and inability to consistently meet their core needs in a way that was aligned with their values.

But she had violated her moral compass and now it was back to haunt her.

Paris Toujours Paris.

DISCLAIMER

Paris Toujours Paris is a work of fiction.

Although its form is that of a semi-autobiography (Gabrielle's) it is not one.

With the exception of public places, any resemblance to persons living or dead is coincidental. Space and time have been rearranged to suit the convenience of the book, memory has its own story to tell.

The opinions expressed are those of the characters and should not be confused with the author's.

AUTHOR'S NOTE

Thank you so much for reading *Paris Toujours Paris.*

I hope you enjoyed this novella as an escapist story, but perhaps you also glimpsed something beneath as you read. A review would be much appreciated as it helps other readers discover the story. Thanks.

If you sign up for my newsletter you'll be notified of giveaways, new releases and receive personal updates from behind the scenes of my business and books.

Go to www.thepeoplealchemist.com to get started.

Places in the book

I have set the story in real places in Paris and in a modelled fictional town in the north of France for *Le PDG* backstory. You can see some of the places here:

- Canonbury Square and Gardens
- Tour Eiffel

- Tour Montparnasse

Bibliography

I read different books as part of my research. Some of them together with other references include:

The Artist Way - **Julia Cameron**
The Complete Reader - **Neville Goddard**, compiled and edited by **David Allen**
Psycho-Cybernetics - **Maxwell Maltz**
A Theory of Human Motivation - **Abraham Maslow**

Printed in Great Britain
by Amazon

83051910R00031